Ghost of Kemiekoo: Untold Story

R.C. Bolden-Wilder

AuthorHouse™
1663 Liberty Drive
Bloomington, IN 47403
www.authorhouse.com
Phone: 1 (800) 839-8640

Published by AuthorHouse 09/19/2018

ISBN: 978-1-5462-5988-6 (sc)
ISBN: 978-1-5462-5987-9 (e)

Library of Congress Control Number: 2018911132

Print information available on the last page.

Any people depicted in stock imagery provided by Getty Images are models,
and such images are being used for illustrative purposes only.
Certain stock imagery © Getty Images.

This book is printed on acid-free paper.

Because of the dynamic nature of the Internet, any web addresses or links contained in this book may have changed
since publication and may no longer be valid. The views expressed in this work are solely those of the author and do
not necessarily reflect the views of the publisher, and the publisher hereby disclaims any responsibility for them.

authorHOUSE®

To my son Maurice,

Always make sure that you fight for what you believe in. If there is something that you're great at don't let anyone else tell you otherwise. Nothing happens overnight. Giving it your all is what matters. Make sure to embrace the failures and you will succeed.

Love you always, Dad

Many know who Kemiekoo is. Father of one. Lived in Mariners Harbor for most of his life. One of the most positive, respected people you'll ever meet. Kind, polite, loves music and of course handsome. But of all things his greatest accomplishment is being the great koolaid maker of all time. Nothing else matters at that point. But what people don't know is: who was the original Kemiekoo?

I know what you're thinking. The man by the name of Eric Swift did not, I repeat did not, come up with the original name "Kemiekoo". Sorry my good man but you are not that guy. Move in closer, turn off the lights and play some spooky music that has that weird, creepy, foggy at night background on. You will now learn the truth of Kemiekoo:

Staten Island; Mariners Harbor

September 18, 1998

Kareem Koomeenie. 17 years old in his senior year of Port Richmond High School. Lived with his older brother Jarod, 38, and Jarod's wife Madilyn, 37 since the passing of there parents. Kareem was 14 when they passed. He just started in Port Richmond High School at the beginning of the school year. After a great first day of school, he came into his building hearing gun shots. He ran inside and heard more from the elevator.

A man ran from the elevator. Kareem was in shock that he tried to ram the gunman, but he grabbed him and lifted Kareem in the air. Before he could toss him, sirens went off and the cops were on their way. He dropped Kareem and left the building.

Kareem was terrified. Such a rush. He walked slowly over to the elevator. As he looked inside, he saw what he hoped he would never see. His mom and dad shot. Not a chance at all of escaping. He dropped down in tears trying to see if one of them were still breathing. Sorry Kareem.

When the cops arrived, they saw what the damage and called the ambulance. People in the building and around the area gave their statements and descriptions of the gunman. The police asked Kareem if there was anyone they could call to come get Kareem. He was in too much shock to reply. Someone who knew the family called Jarod to come to the station and get him. While at the station Kareem used whatever memory to describe the gunman. Kareem remembered where he saw him in the past. The guy used to try and take his mom away from his father. His mom was always faithful to her husband, but the guy never gave up. One can only think that seeing them in the elevator why not get them and make sure they could never be happy. So sad.

Staten Island; Mariners Harbor

October 13th, 2001

Years after his parent's murder, Kareem is still hurt inside but doesn't talk about it at all. He continued with his life. Friends have came and gone. Even had a few girlfriends since. Very popular in his neighborhood and stays out of trouble. Seems like a good kid, right?

Few days later, it was announced that there was a drink maker competition where the winner would win $10,000. If they made the best drink ever. Kareem's friends told him about it and he joined in. How could he pass up such an opportunity? One of his greatest talents of course he's going to want to show off.

It was Halloween and time for the NYC Drink Makers competition right in his neighborhood. Drink makers from all over New York and different ages. So much at stake: the money, fame and plus Hot 97 was there. The hottest radio station in NY at the time. Judges were walking around from table to table. Trying all the different types of drinks: alcohol, seltzer, soda, sparkling water you name it. I'm telling you this event was huge. Then came Kareem's turn......

The judges walked over. Talked to him for a bit. After that was done, they each picked up a cup. Different flavors but same drink. They spit it all out. They were disgusted. Unimpressed. They moved along and there goes his shot. But how could they not like it? What was the issue? He wondered and took a taste. It was undoubtedly off. But it wasn't like that before the competition. Seconds later he had a horrible taste in his mouth. He then dropped on the floor hitting his head on his table. Someone saw and called the ambulance. Few minutes later when they arrived Kareem was gone, and nobody knew why up to this day.

Staten Island; Mariners Harbor

October 13th, 2011

10 years has passed since the competition. Not even a winner was crowned. Few were disappointed, but many understood. But as we all know there is a new Kemiekoo that has been around for many years. Very few knew about the original Koo. It was kept a secret for a while.

Flyers were being placed around the hood about the 2nd annual NYC Drink Maker Contest. Now of course it caught the attention of one Rahkeem Bolden, new Kemiekoo. 21 years of age. He has taken this name and drink to new levels. Koo cubes, koomixes (songs). Selling them in gallons, cups, quarts and even Gatorade containers. People he has 99 flavas and chalk ain't one. Feel me? From Delaware to New York to New Jersey. Can you blame the guy for his success?

He went over to the community center across the street to sign up. Now this is the hood. You'll see your normal homeless, crackheads, drug addicts, drug dealers and more. There was one in particular in between buildings close to the community center laying up against one of the gates. He tried to get Rahkeem's attention but Rahkeem has his headphones on and once he has that, well he's just like everyone else with headphones. Leave the man alone. The guys name is R.E.D. Red-Eyed Dave. Appears to have been there at the first competition. According to him, he claims that he has seen Kareem's ghost as well.

On the way back home, he was walking past R.E.D. and he grabbed Rahkeem's arm: "YOU WILL NEVER BE AS GOOD AS HE WAS!!!! HE WILL RETURN!!!! BEWARE BOY!!!!" Rahkeem had chills inside of him. Kind of a creepy chilling feeling. Times like that you might want to listen and prepare. Rahkeem told his friends what happened. Its not the first time R.E.D. has told people this. But what they couldn't understand is: why did he appear now more than ever unless he was telling the truth? Crazy nightmares for days Rahkeem had about the ghost and R.E.D.'s warning. When he couldn't sleep he did his research. A man needs to be prepared since he listened.

The day has come. Its time for the 2nd Annual NYC Drink Makers contest. A lot more people were interested. Still for the same amount of money. This time the news reporters were involved. Almost every radio station was there as well. Law enforcement too. People believe they will see a ghost and great competition. A lot of people had their "Kemiekoo" signs up. Not sure for which one though.

So much attention. He has had people congratulate him or even thanked him for great things he has done. But no camera crew or even signs up for nothing crazy. The man became nervous. Unsure if he wanted to carry on. He knew he had to pull himself together. His table was set with everything. From the Koo to the KooCubes. Three different flavas with the different flavored cubes. As the judges started walking there was a change in the sky. Such a dark gray to have you thinking that a crazy storm was coming. Contest was far from coming to an end. They wanted a winner.

The judges were finally walking towards Rahkeem. He turned to check on his drinks and R.E.D. was there crouched under his arm. Rahkeem looked confused. Before he could question, the judges appeared at the table. He turned around to face the judges and welcome them. Then turned and saw that R.E.D. was gone. Strange but that's how it goes. The judges had a talk with Rahkeem explaining to him that they were the original judges from 10 years ago. That he was not the first to claim this name. He understood and was sure to still win in the original Koo honor. Time for them to taste.

The cameras were close on everything. As they picked up their glasses and cups getting closer to there mouths, the extra cup that he left for himself began to rise from the table. Everyone began to step back. Some of them took off and started running. The glass then turned upside down and poured out the Koo that was inside. Small gusts of winds started to form in the center of the competition. Lightning appeared and destroyed the lens of all the cameras and took out all the phones. The gusts of winds formed into a small miniature whirlwind. Lightning struck in the whirlwind as the GHOST OF KEMIEKOO arose from the dead.

Everyone began to run in fear. Table flew, lightning was all over and people running in terror for their lives. The ghost saw Rahkeem trying to leave the wind pulled only him in. A little whirlwind picked him up and constricted him, so he couldn't get away. There he was. Eye to eye with the one who was the original before he was Kemiekoo. He was scared like I don't know what. But he had answers. Answers that he knew would solve all.

He first apologized for taking his name. He was unaware that someone had the name before him and he apologizes. He then explained that he knew what happened to the contest and to him. He did his research and realized that the same person who tried to sabotage him was the same one who sabotaged and killed him years ago. Red Eyed Dave aka R.E.D. also known as Dave Brickman. ONE of the sons of the name that killed Kareem's parents, Brian Brickman. He poisoned the drink of his right after the judges tried the drinks that he tampered with before the competition started. He did it for revenge of sending his father to jail. He didn't care why he went. He just wanted revenge. He went homeless after his father went to jail and appeared around more after he saw Kareem's ghost in his dreams and then the flyers of the contest.

The ghost became furious. He let Rahkeem go and sent the winds to bring R.E.D. to him. Sadly for R.E.D. he wasn't fast enough, and he was close by. He was dragged all the way to the center of the whirlwind screaming in fear. Once the ghost had him, the winds, the ghost and R.E.D. just disappeared with no trace anywhere. Since then there was only one man named Kemiekoo and that man will forever be Rahkeem Bolden. Goodnight all.

Printed in the United States
By Bookmasters